Mother Mule

By CAITLYN WALLINGER

Illustrated by Kelcey Jones

EAST 26TH
PUBLISHING

Wes—
I am forever grateful you picked me out of the 'crowd'
all those years ago. Thank you for creating this life with me, and for
always believing in me, even when I don't believe in myself. I love you.

Max & Levi—
Being your Mom is my life's greatest gift and fondest adventure.
I hope you always remember to look for magic, and to chase your dreams.
I love you more than you'll ever know.

Mother Mule

Copyright © 2020 by Caitlyn Wallinger

Libary of Congress Cataloging-in-Publication data is available
ISBN: 978-1-7348856-1-3

Editing, book layout and cover by Krista Huber
Typography is Cormorant set in size 14

10 9 8 7 6 5 4 3 2 1
First printing edition 2020

East 26th Publishing
Houston, TX

www.east26thpublishing.com

Matthew 11:28-30

Come to me, all you who are weary and burdened, and I will give you rest. Take my yoke upon you and learn from me, for I am gentle and humble in heart, and you will find rest for your souls. For my yoke is easy and my burden is light.

This is Mother Mule.
She spends her days tending to her family
while carrying their belongings in her pack.

Mother Mule and Daddy Mule
have two little boys—
Brother Mule and Baby Mule.

The family lives in a small red
barn on a quiet plot of land.

There is a creek nearby where
the boys fish for *crabhogs* and
throw rocks.

Daddy Mule helps the boys create fishing rods out of sticks.
He ties twine to one end and attaches a piece of salami to the other.
Daddy loves salami, and he's sure *crabhogs* do too.

Mother Mule goes about her days with her pockets full of her family's favorite things.
She wears a colorful satchel that Daddy gave her on their wedding day.

In it, she keeps:

Her favorite lotion (her hooves are always dry from washing throughout the day),
Daddy Mule's sunglasses (she has to keep them safe from little sticky hooves),
Brother Mule's toys (he would bring his entire toy bin with him if he could!),
and Baby Mule's favorite snacks (he is a picky eater and grazes all day long!).

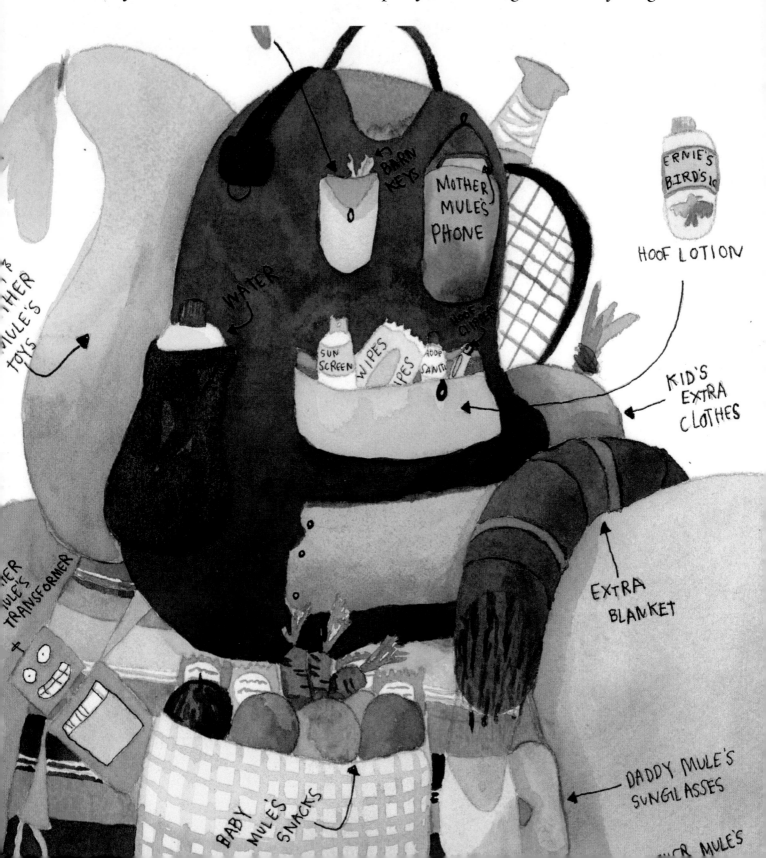

There are so many things to carry, and she can't leave the barn without any of them.

One day, as the family left for their errands, Brother Mule left his new transforming robot on the bench by the barn door. He was so upset, Mother Mule had to gallop all the way back to the barn to get it.

By the time she made it back to Brother, Baby, and Daddy, the boys were hungry for lunch. So, they had to forget about their errands and head back home.

After that day, Mother Mule always checked her pockets before leaving the barn.

Mother Mule's pack is quite heavy with the weight of all of her family's treasures. It makes her sleepy, and her hooves sore. Her shoulders slouch as she moves. There are always more and more toys and snacks to carry.

One day, while Mother Mule carried out her chores for the day, she came across a glimmering pool of water.

As she marveled from afar, it beckoned her closer.

Nearing the water, she realized how thirsty she was, having left her favorite water bottle back at the barn.
Mother Mule bent down to take a thirsty drink, but quickly jumped backwards when she noticed a bright smile greeting her.
Then, a soft voice spoke out.
Mother Mule! I've been waiting for you. Please, take a rest beside me.

But Mother Mule couldn't take a rest!

She had to gather food for dinner (it was pasta night).
She had toys to clean up
(the boys' room looked like a hurricane blew through it).
And she just realized she hadn't brushed her teeth yet today!
Brother Mule and Baby Mule would be home from school soon.
They would be hungry and wanting her to play with them.

Mother Mule simply could not slow down.

The soft voice spoke again,
*Mother Mule! Sit. Breathe.
I am here to help; please accept my offer.*
The calm voice created soothing
ripples in the pool of water, and
Mother Mule felt her body relax.

The special pockets full of her family's treasures
jingled as she lowered herself to the ground.
She breathed slowly and talked with the magic pool of water while munching on
one of Baby Mule's snack bars, realizing she had not eaten anything all day!

The smiling pool of water told Mother Mule of
a secret treasure hidden within the water's depths.
It was a golden rock, and it had powers.

Mother Mule looked deep into the calm water,
her eyes widening when she saw the glittering
golden rock below.

The water explained that its magic is only visible to those who truly
believe, and, in order for it to work, she must make a promise.
A beam of sunlight sent a sparkle across the surface of the water.

What promise? Mother Mule asked.

You must promise to always ask for help whenever you need it.
The face in the pool of water held Mother Mule's gaze as it spoke these words.

Mother Mule made her promise and reached down
into the cool blue water to pull out the rock.
"This can't be a rock!" she exclaimed. "It's light as a feather!"

Yes, the soft voice replied.
*And it will fit perfectly in one
of your special pockets.*

Mother Mule really
didn't want any more
things to carry, but
she was drawn to the
beauty and mystery of
the golden rock and its
powers.

So, Mother Mule dropped it into one of her pockets.

Her pack, weighted down with all her family's treasures, suddenly became light as a feather, just like the golden rock!

The smiling pool of water gave Mother Mule a wink and disappeared, leaving nothing but a dry patch of land behind.

Mother Mule sat quietly for a few moments, in awe of what she had just witnessed. Then, she looked down where the pool of water had been only moments before, and laughed— a pure, joyful laugh.

Rising from the ground, she went on her way to get fixings for dinner,
and to tidy up the family's barn before picking up the boys from school.

She skipped, jumped, and hopped through the tall grass, enjoying the new weightlessness of her pack. She felt so thankful for the generous offering from the magic pool of water, glad she accepted its help.

That evening, as Mother Mule prepared
dinner, she told her family of the magic pool
of water and the gift of the golden rock.

Brother Mule and Baby Mule gasped as Mother Mule explained the magic it possessed, examining it carefully.

"Soft!" said Baby Mule.

"It's so sparkly!" Brother Mule smiled.

As Mother Mule placed the golden stone back into her pocket, she told Brother and Baby how helping others spreads magic, just like the rock.

After dinner, Daddy Mule cleaned the dishes and packed lunches for the next day.

Brother and Baby tidied their room and helped one another get into their favorite matching pajamas. Mother Mule peeked into their room and smiled as she witnessed the simple kindness.

She and Daddy Mule gathered Brother and Baby into a great big group hug. "Always be helpers," Mother Mule said, "Even if nobody asks. You never know how much offering to help can mean to someone who is struggling."

Mother Mule never took the magic
golden rock out of her pocket.
Her pack was always light as a feather,
no matter what she carried.

She kept her promise to the
magic pool of water, too.

She asked Daddy to help with meals
when she wasn't feeling well.

She asked her neighbors to pick up the
boys when she was running late.

By asking for help from her family and friends, she could take better care of her loved ones, helping them in return.

She felt happy and rested now, rather than tired and heavy all the time. Her family noticed these changes, too. Brother Mule liked the new way Mother styled her mane, and that she now wore pretty pink stuff on her lips.

Mother Mule also made sure to share the magic of the rock, by helping her fellow mothers whenever they needed it, whether they asked or not.

Nowadays, you can always find Mother Mule with a few extra belongings in her special pockets.

Made in the USA
Coppell, TX
08 March 2021